SNEAKERS

by Ray Anthony Shepard

Random House/New York

To Mom and Boots, who suggested
the names for some of the characters

Cover illustrations/Richard Sparks

Copyright © 1973 by Ray Anthony Shepard

All rights reserved under International
and Pan-American Copyright Conventions.
Published in the United States by Random House, Inc.,
New York.

Library of Congress Catalog Card Number: 79-65159
ISBN: 0-394-62057-7
This edition published by arrangement with
E. P. Dutton & Co. Inc.

Manufactured in the United States of America
9 8 7 6 5 4 3 2 1
Random House Student Book Program Edition:
First Printing, October, 1979

CHAPTER ONE

It was a bright, late October afternoon. The sun hung in the blue sky over the stubbly green grass. Large metal H's stood at each end of the field like strange scarecrows from a faraway land. Down below, behind a new yellow brick school, boys in plastic helmets, brown canvas pants, and puffed-shoulder sweat shirts ran back and forth over the white-striped football field.

G.L. broke out of the huddle first and ran up to the ball. The rest of the line joined him. Chuck, the right end, dug his feet in the grass as he settled into his stance. His knuckles were reddish brown as they nudged into position. Craig stood over the center and barked the signals, "Ready, set, hut one, hut two, hut three."

G.L. snapped the ball. Craig faked a hand-off to Leonard, the running back, and then stepped into his pocket. Chuck ran straight ahead for ten yards. The defensive back picked him up. Chuck faked his head to the outside and made a sharp cut to the inside. The defender took the fake and went to the outside. Chuck's hands waited for the ball, but it was no use. The ball was high and to the outside. It

3

bounced helplessly on the ground and out of bounds.

He walked slowly back to the huddle. "Man, when are you going to learn to throw the ball?" Chuck asked, throwing down his helmet.

Craig unbuttoned his chin strap, his eyes locked with Chuck's. "When are you going to learn to run your patterns right?"

Chuck's sandy brown Afro stood up straight after he ran his hand over his head to wipe away the sweat. "I was supposed to cut to the inside."

"No, you weren't."

"You're always messing up my plays!"

"Liar!" Craig said.

Chuck doubled up his fists. "What did you say?"

"You heard me." Then he shouted again, "Liar!" When he shouted this time, he did it with his mouth wide open. Chuck could see past his teeth, past the red meaty insides, even way down to the darkness of his throat.

"What do you want me to do next time, hand-carry the ball to you?" Craig asked with scorn.

The anger rose in Chuck. "I just wish you could learn to throw the ball," he yelled. "And if you call me a liar one more time, I'm going to beat your old white hide so bad . . ." He was so mad he couldn't find the words to end the sentence; instead he bent down and grabbed a rock.

There was silence. Four eyes locked together, while the rest of the players looked on, waiting. Chuck squeezed the rock tighter.

"What do you need the rock for?"

4

"For your head, if you keep messing with me."

As if they had all seen the same western on TV, the two teams stepped back.

"Both of you are going to be in trouble when the coach gets back," G.L. said, but he stepped back too.

Suddenly it was only Chuck and Craig. One of them had to make his play.

"If you want to fight, okay, I'll fight you. I'm not afraid of you. Put the rock down and we'll see whose head you're going to beat on!" Craig clenched his fists and bit his bottom lip. "Is that how you fight?"

"I'll fight any way I choose!"

"You got the rock because you're afraid."

"And you're going to know about this rock if you don't shut up."

"You're just scared, that's all. Just like you got to lie all the time." Craig stopped biting his lip and opened his mouth wider, showing more of the meaty insides. "You liar." And then he said the words that pulled the trigger, and it was said so the whole world could hear it. "YOU BLACK NIGGER LIAR!"

Chuck threw the rock as hard as he could, shouting, "I told you to watch your mouth."

Craig grabbed his shoulder and Chuck moved in on him, sending his bony brown fist against Craig's white teeth.

Craig pushed him back with both hands and kicked him on the leg, shouting from behind blood-stained teeth, "You've asked for it. Come on!"

But Chuck didn't rush him. He danced around with his fists doubled, waiting for his chance to charge.

"Not so big without a rock," Craig called.

"If you guys are going to fight, then fight, will you!" someone yelled.

"Go on and get him, Chuck, nobody else is going to get into this," Leonard assured his friend.

Then Craig started dancing around too. They circled each other, waiting for a chance. Craig made his move. He jumped forward. Chuck tried to back away, but somehow Craig was able to grab him around the neck. As they twisted and grunted, Chuck moved his feet between Craig's and they fell to the ground.

They rolled to the right, then to the left. First Craig was on top, then Chuck. Craig ended back on top and started pounding Chuck's head against the ground.

"Get off!" Chuck yelled, knowing he would have to do something more than yell. He started to buck up and down, until Craig fell off. Chuck quickly rolled after him, sending his feet into Craig's stomach. It didn't hurt Craig much, because they were both on the ground, but it kept him away.

"Get him good, Chuck," G.L. urged as he, too, started dancing around, throwing make-believe punches in the air.

Someone shouted encouragement to Craig, and the rest of the team yelled and screamed.

Craig tried to kick back. When he did, it was easy for Chuck to grab his leg and twist. Craig pulled away and they both got to their feet. Blood still trickled from the front of Craig's mouth. Dirt was caked in Chuck's hair. His head throbbed and there was a scratch on the side of his face.

On their feet again, they circled each other. Craig sent a left jab that caught Chuck on the ear. The team was shouting louder, wanting to see more blood. The anger in Chuck continued to grow, because he knew he wasn't winning. The fight was too even. The anger grew so strong that he gave up circling. He stopped waiting for the right opening and just charged blindly. They both fell to the ground again. As Chuck tried to roll to the left, Craig stuck a fist in his stomach. They struggled until Chuck was on top and Craig held his arms desperately.

CHAPTER TWO

"All right! What's the trouble here?"

Chuck saw giant white shoes standing near him. There was only one pair of size thirteen feet in the whole school. It had to be Big Mac.

"On your feet." Craig immediately dropped Chuck's arms, causing him to fall to one side. "All right," Big Mac repeated, "which one of you started it? What's it all about?" he demanded as they stood up.

Mr. MacDonald, the gym teacher, stood staring for a long time, as if trying to make them wish they weren't there. "The rest of you boys get out of here," he ordered the team onlookers. "Clear out. The circus is over." They started to move slowly. They were too slow for Big Mac, so he shouted again, "I said move, and that's just what I mean." They moved a little faster.

When the rest of the team had gone, Big Mac asked again. "What's this all about?" Craig rocked back and forth on his heels. Neither boy answered. The coach waited. Still there was no answer.

Big Mac unzipped his jacket and put his hands on his hips. His chest swelled as he demanded, "I know you heard me. What's going on? Talk!"

The two boys looked at each other, each wondering who was going to tell on whom first.

"This is the last time I'm asking." Chuck could tell he was getting madder. His ears were turning red, which made his face seem whiter and meaner. "How did it start?" Still no answer. "I'll tell you what we can do, since you don't want to talk. We'll finish this fight right here. Just you two, and I'll let you fight until you can't fight anymore."

"He's always complaining," Craig said.

"I'm not, you're the one."

"He threw a rock at me."

"Liar!"

"You're the liar."

"Hold it, just hold on. One at a time," Big Mac said. Then Craig offered his side of the story. The coach listened, moving his head up and down on every other word. When Craig finished, Big Mac asked Chuck for his version. He told him. The coach said nothing, just nodded on every other word. Chuck was sure Craig would be agreed with, because Craig was white. Chuck promised himself that he wasn't finished with Craig. There would be other times.

Big Mac looked at both of them. He zipped his jacket back up and started moving his mouth slowly, up and down in a lazy motion. "Fighting doesn't do any good for either of you. It's not going to make you play better football. It's only going to hurt you. Both of you have to work together. You're on the same team and you need each other; that is, if either of you is interested in seeing the eighth grade beat the ninth." Then his ears got red again. His mouth moved faster and his words shot out. "And here are my two best players out fighting each other. You two are supposed to be helping the rest of the team get ready and what are you doing? Helping? No! You got the rest of the team watching you fight, watching my best players roll in the dirt."

Craig and Chuck looked at their feet, each wanting to melt into the grass. Anything that would free them from Big Mac's wrath.

"Coach Price will be glad to know that my team would prefer to fight each other, rather than his guys. Okay, get to the showers."

In the locker room the rest of the team was coming out of the showers. Some were already dressed. Craig went off to his locker, which was at one end, and a group of guys joined him. G.L. and Leonard, whose lockers were on either side of Chuck's, waited for him.

"What did Big Mac say?" Leonard asked.

"You know. The same old jive."

"It figures. Teachers never change their line."

G.L. held his stomach in and stuck out his chest like the coach. "You two boys, I mean men, better try to work together, for this here football game. After all, brotherhood week is coming up."

"Yeah, that's just how it went."

"Well, it's time for me to went," said Leonard. "Got to get to the library. Got to do a silly book report or something. You coming with me, G.L.?"

"Yeah, I'm coming. And Chuck, you better put it in second if you're going to make the bus."

"I've got plenty of time."

"You'll have plenty of time if you have to walk fifteen miles to get home."

"I'll see you guys on the bus."

Chuck started to untie his sneakers. They played in regular football uniforms except for shoes. Instead they wore their gym shoes. He stared down at them, wishing they were football shoes, with cleats so he wouldn't have to worry about slipping and he could make his cuts sharper.

"With some real ones, I could show them. I wouldn't have to worry about messing up in front of everybody," Chuck mumbled to himself, worried about how he would play in the game. He had just untied one sneaker when Big Mac came into the locker room. He walked in his office and came right back out.

"Chuck," Big Mac called, then he called for Craig.

Now what, Chuck thought. I wish he'd leave it alone.

Chuck got there first, then Craig came in. The office was very small, more like a closet or a telephone booth. There was hardly room for three with the desk, chair, and a locker all stuffed into that little room. Chuck stood next to the locker and watched Big Mac write something down on a piece of paper, rather than look at Craig. When Big Mac finished, he looked up and frowned. There was silence. Finally he said, "Craig, Chuck, I want you two to be game captains. What about it?"

"But, Coach, you told me I was going to be the captain," Craig answered.

There was a pause, and Big Mac's ears turned red. "Craig, you're still going to be a captain. I just want Chuck to be one with you. Chuck, how do you feel about it?"

"I don't know." Church shrugged his shoulders.

"Why not? Don't you think you can help lead the team?"

"Maybe. Maybe not."

"Don't you want to be co-captain with Craig?"

"Craig doesn't bother me none."

"Maybe he wants to be captain by himself," Craig said with a smirk on his face.

"Okay, I'll show you, wise guy. Yeah, I'll be a captain."

"Good. Now that's all settled." Big Mac smiled. Craig had a hurt frown on his face and a small

11

smile sneaked from the side of Chuck's mouth as he looked at him.

Chuck went back to his locker. Everyone else had dressed and gone. It was almost time for the second bus to leave. He did have to hurry. He untied his sneakers for the second time and suddenly they looked terrible. There was a small tear in the left one. Both were dirty gray from sweat.

"With some cleats, I'd be able to do my stuff. I don't see why this dumb school got us wearing tennis shoes like we were babies," he complained to himself. Disgusted, he sat there and looked down at his feet.

As he stared, he tried to move his toes. The more he stared at the ragged, sweat-stained sneakers, the harder it was to wiggle his toes. "And they're too small!" he said to the empty room.

Chuck was undressed and heading for the shower before the idea of getting a new pair of sneakers occurred to him.

"Yeah, that's it!" he said out loud again.

His mind started to click, his eyes clouded over, and things seemed quite clear to him. With new ones he would be able to run faster. Then nobody would be able to catch him. The soles would be new and they would stick to the ground and he wouldn't have to worry about slipping. Even if Craig threw to the wrong side, he would be quick enough to get the ball anyway. That would show Craig; he would really be sick then.

His dreaming stopped when he realized there was no way he was going to get some new shoes. His mother had said the old ones had to last the

12

rest of the school year, and here it was only October.

Taking his shower, he couldn't help but think about the game with the ninth grade. He just knew he was the best end in the whole school. He knew he could run and catch better than the guys in the ninth. And with some new sneakers he would be even better. The eighth would win just because of him. From this game, high school coaches from all over the city would hear about him. They would want him to think about coming to their school in a year. He would become a high school star, then a college all-American, and eventually a pro.

He stood there under the water, thinking how nice it would be to be a pro. He could do soap commercials after the games. If you were going to be a pro and make commercials, it was good to start out by being a game captain and not messing up in front of everybody. Then he wondered if he would have to do soap commercials without any clothes on. Well, he decided, he wouldn't do them if you couldn't wear something to cover yourself. He would do one for foot powder. That would be better. At least you could do it in your underwear, and that was bad enough.

CHAPTER THREE

The bus was still waiting when Chuck came out of
the gym. When he saw that the engine hadn't even
been started, he slowed his walk. G.L. and Leonard
were standing by the door talking to some of the
other guys. Chuck shivered a little when he felt the
air. His hair was still a little wet from the shower,
so he pulled his red felt cap tight around his head
and tried to blow smoke to test just how cold it
was, but not much came out. He knew it was getting colder, even if he couldn't see his breath too
well. It was the kind of late afternoon that meant
football season was about over.

Now that G.L. and Leonard were with the rest
of their friends and already knew that Big Mac
hadn't given Chuck too much flak, they greeted
Chuck like a hero. Of course it made them feel like
heroes, or at least friends of a hero, since they had
been there and had seen everything.

"Man, that was some fight, Chuck," G.L. said.
"You should have seen how he did that old white
boy in." Then he danced on his toes and threw a
couple of punches, demonstrating how it had been
to those who were unfortunate enough to have
missed it.

While G.L. gave a replay of the fight, Leonard

walked over and grabbed Chuck's hand, pumping it up and down. "That was some fight, but for a minute there, I thought he was going to do you in."

Chuck jerked his hand away. "What do you mean? Craig didn't stand a chance against me." He waited, making sure he had everybody's attention. "Anyway, I beat on the dude's head so bad, the coach wants me to be a captain."

"Wow, that's something. So Big Mac has gone and integrated his captains. He must really need us," G.L. told them with surprising seriousness.

And Leonard joined him. "Of course he needs us! The eighth grade hasn't beaten the ninth in five years. This will be the first time, if we do it."

There was a slight frown on Chuck's face. He was disappointed that they didn't see his being a co-captain in the same way that he saw it. He tried to straighten them out. "Well, we'll beat them. Just leave it to me."

"You going to do it by yourself?" Leonard asked him. Then he said to the rest of the guys, "It's the first year they've been busing us out here, right? So I guess Big Mac decided he was going to get some-thing out of all this busing."

The rest of the group nodded their heads in agreement. Brother said he knew why Craig was so sore today. Brother was too fat to play any sport, but he made up for it by knowing everything that went on in the school.

"He was mad because he knew I was getting more of the limelight than he was," Chuck put in. "Now I will for sure."

15

Brother moved closer to Chuck. "No, no, that ain't all of it. He was mad at all of you guys even before he came on the field. In fact, he's mad at every black kid in the school."

"Why?"

"Because he got hustled out of his lunch money!" Whenever Brother gave out information, he did it with authority, and with the enjoyment of someone who tasted authority rarely.

"By who?"

"Who else?" Brother answered with raised eyebrows. "Alvin and his little group."

It was Chuck's turn to step up to Brother. "I don't care if they took all of his money. I didn't take it, so he doesn't have to get mad with me. Anyway, I've been having trouble with him before, so he's just using that as an excuse to cover up his real thing. He can think we're all in it together, because that's the way his head thinks. He can think the way he wants to, but he just better stay out of my way."

"But he's your co-captain, Captain Walker," G.L. said and started laughing, which made everybody but Chuck laugh.

The driver started the engine, and they climbed onto the bus. There was a lot of noise inside. Chuck looked for a seat by himself. His head was hurting, and although he hadn't mentioned it, it was beginning to bother him more. Nobody was taking him seriously enough anyway, so he would sit alone.

CHAPTER FOUR

No sooner had he found a seat by the window than he heard, "Chuck, Chuck, are you hurt?" It was Thelma coming on the bus. She was out of breath from running, yet her voice was loud and clear. "Tell me all about it," she yelled as she hurried up the aisle, holding a pile of books that threatened to bounce from her arms.

Thelma dropped down next to Chuck, causing all the air to push out of the ripped seat like air rushing out of an untied balloon. Before the cotton stuffing settled or she could rearrange her books, the questions came.

"Did you get hurt? Is the whole school talking about your fight? I wanted to be there. Why didn't you have the fight when I was there? What was it about? Did he hurt you?"

Chuck forgot about his headache. He pulled himself up in his seat and spoke in his deepest voice. "Craig couldn't have hurt me, even if he tried."

"Tell me all about it. I want to know everything." She wiggled in her seat, trying to put her books in an orderly stack.

Still in a deep voice that strained much lower

this time, Chuck said, "You can see the next one, because I'm not through with him yet."

"God, you might need me there!"

"For what?" Another frown raced across his face.

"I can make sure he doesn't try to throw any sneaky punches. Besides, I can fight too, you know."

By now the frown had won and his head was hurting again. "Yeah, sure. You're subject to miss it, like you almost missed the bus. Maybe you can come and throw books at Craig."

"Okay, wise guy. Go on and get hit with a couple of sneaky punches. See if I care." That was the end of their conversation.

Chuck lived next door to Thelma, and their mothers had been friends for years. Chuck thought Thelma was always trying to act like his big sister, which he didn't need or want. The rest of the kids who rode the bus thought Thelma and Chuck were going together. That's what Chuck wanted, but she was always acting too stupid for that. Even when he tried to be nice to her, she would come on like she was taking care of him.

He really wished they were going together, because now was the time, he reasoned. She did look good. He enjoyed the way the rest of the guys thought he had her all locked up, even if he didn't. She was thirteen with big brown eyes and a large Afro. A lot of the other girls were jealous of her, but she didn't pay much attention to them. Thelma always did what she wanted, without having to wait around and see what the other girls were going to do.

That's not necessarily what Chuck liked about her. What he did like was the way she looked and the way they would look together. The best football player with the best-looking girl. That's how it should be. Chuck just wished she would act like his girl, and besides, she could help him with his homework.

The bus was on the highway. In a while it would be puffing as fast as it could, which wasn't very fast. Soon there wouldn't be very many small houses. There would be big buildings on top of big buildings and cars on top of cars. There would be very few white faces. Instead there would be yellow-black faces, brown-black faces, and black-black faces. They would be home.

Chuck's mother had told him how lucky he was to be going to a good school. But to Chuck it meant getting up early and getting home late. Just a long bus ride to be bored in school, just like he was bored when he didn't have to get up so early, or ride a bus to school. Right now, however, as the bus got closer to home, he was glad to be getting away from the Craigs and the Mr. MacDonalds for another day.

As the bus got closer to Boston, Thelma tried to talk to Chuck again. She asked if he had heard what Alvin was up to. Chuck reminded her sarcastically that since she could defend herself, she wouldn't have to worry over Alvin.

When she tried to talk to him about their English class, he didn't even say a sarcastic word. She knew he had only read the first chapter of *Manchild in the Promised Land*, and they were supposed to be halfway through it now. But Chuck was hopelessly behind, and he didn't want to be reminded of his plight. When she asked him if he was ready for the football game, he stopped looking out the window and gave a simple "No."

"Why not?" she asked with real concern.

Her words softened him. He was beginning to feel glad he had allowed himself to continue their conversation. "My shoes ain't right."

"What's wrong with them?"

"They're too small. They're so tight I can't run right."

Thelma thought about it for a minute. "You better be glad you got some everyday shoes that fit your fat feet," she said, looking down at his loafers. "Some of the kids on this bus don't even have that. And here you are worrying about some new tennis shoes. You can run just as fast in those old ones."

Chuck sighed, his shoulders sunk, and he slid down in his seat. "No, I can't." He spoke halfheartedly from his slouched position.

By now the bus had reached Roxbury, the black section of Boston. Brother got off at the first stop. Leonard and G.L. got off at Dudley Station, and when the bus stopped at the shopping center on Warren Street, Thelma and Chuck got off in silence.

"Well, if you think you have to have them, maybe you better find a job," Thelma suggested as they cut through one of the stores.

"What good would that do? Even if I could find one, I wouldn't get the money in time. Friday is only three days from now. What kind of job would pay me before I did the work?"

"I'm just trying to help. You don't have to get so sore."

"You're always trying to help! If you wouldn't act so silly, I wouldn't have to get mad."

They reached the Markdale Housing Project, located behind the shopping center.

Thelma sighed. "This has been some day, and there's more to come. I got to go right in and eat because I got a job baby-sitting for a lady in the next building."

"I thought your mother didn't let you baby-sit on school nights?"

"I'm going to buy a typewriter. Mother knows how bad I need one. All the white kids turn in their homework typed. Well, I can too! Daddy said there's one down at a pawnshop for only twenty dollars. I only have to sit for a couple of hours until the baby's father gets off work. I'll make a dollar a day. Mother said I could do it for a month. By that time I'll have the twenty dollars."

"Sure wish I could find me some kids to take care of. You girls have it made. There's always somebody's kids to be looked after."

"Are you going to do your homework tonight?" she asked.

"Who knows," Chuck said with a nervous grin. "Maybe I'll come over and sit with you!"

"Never happen! I'm not losing my typewriter over your foolishness. And that's just what it would be if my mother ever thought you were anywhere near me when she didn't know about it."

He knew she was going to say no. She never understood anything, he consoled himself. But they were in junior high, and she should stop acting like a little girl.

When they were in front of Thelma's door, she said, "Don't spend too much time thinking about those shoes. You'll run fine in the old ones. No game can be that important anyway. See you tomorrow."

CHAPTER FIVE

Chuck swung open the door and hurried into his house. He was determined to have the sneakers and this was the only place he figured he stood a chance of getting them.

"Mama!" he yelled.

"I'm in the kitchen, Chuck. Why are you busting in this house, screaming like a madman? Haven't I told you about that before?"

"I just wanted to know if you were home," he said, marching into the kitchen.

"Where else would I be?" She had a slight smile on her face.

Chuck had decided that his mother might have

some money that he didn't know about, and he had to find out. But instead of just asking her, or explaining his situation, he would move on it slowly. He had a plan. First he would take the garbage down, and then after dinner he could help with the dishes. He even thought briefly about cleaning up his room, but decided that would be taking things too far.

"How was school today?"

He pulled out a kitchen chair and sat down, shrugging his shoulders. His mother had a dark-brown face, and her hair was black with tiny gray patches that looked something like snow. Chuck always found her face warm, even when she said times were hard. Times had been hard for her the last two years, but she had to believe that things would improve because there was nothing else to believe.

"Did you have a good day, Chuck?" Her voice was cheerful.

"Sure. The same thing goes on all the time." There was no need to tell her about the fight. He knew she wouldn't understand, because she didn't like for him to fight. She never really understood that sometimes he just had to.

Chuck sat at the table playing with a fork, waiting until there was a good time to ask her. "What kind of a day did you have?" he asked.

"Like yours! Same things go on here all the time too." His mother stared at him suspiciously. Chuck smiled back. Then she stopped what she was doing and came over to him. "Okay, young man, what is it? What do you want?"

"Nothing. Can't I even say hello to my own mother?"

"Sure you can. In fact, I'm glad to have somebody to talk to. I'm just used to you running in after school, changing your clothes, and running out again. That's what I'm used to. I'm a little surprised that today you have time to visit with me."

"I don't feel like shooting any baskets. I got to rest. Anyway, it's football season. I got to keep my mind on football."

"And," she said, walking back over to the stove.

"And, it's too cold to go out. Besides, it will be dark out soon, anyway."

"And," she repeated.

"And?" He looked at her, confused. "And that's it."

"We'll see," she said with a slight smile again. She dropped a couple of eggs into a bowl and started beating the mixture with a wooden spoon. Chuck got out the old iron skillet she used for baking cornbread and watched her pour the yellow batter in.

When the bread was in the oven, she started washing out the bowl. "Well, since you're going to stay in and talk to me, I thought maybe we could have supper a little earlier tonight."

"Okay with me," Chuck agreed eagerly.

"But first go change your clothes. I want you to keep your things looking nice for school. I don't want them folks out there thinking we can't afford any decent clothes."

When he returned from changing, he decided

now was the time to begin phase one of Operation Sneakers. "I'll take the garbage down." His mother gave him a surprised look, but said nothing. When they sat down to supper, Chuck began to spread his net that would trap her.

"Mama, Big Mac, I mean, Mr. MacDonald, wants me to be one of the team captains for Friday's game."

"That's nice," She kept on eating.

"The game's Friday."

"Isn't it about time for football to be over? Seems like it's been going on for a long time, or at least you've been talking about it for a long time."

"This is the last game. That's why it's important." He put down his knife, watching to see how she was taking it.

"Eat the rest of your supper before it gets cold. Can't you talk and eat at the same time?"

"Well, I just wanted to tell you about the game. You always want to know what I'm doing in school, so I'm telling you."

"Tell me how you're doing in your classes, then."

"Okay, okay, I guess."

"You guess? Don't you know? How is your English, and what about your math? Are you getting better at it? It seems like you never have any homework to do."

"The teachers out there don't give us a lot of homework to do. I do most of mine at school." That wasn't much of a lie, because he was going to get Thelma to help him. She always had hers done, anyway.

25

"Well, it sure couldn't be much if you have time to play football and do your homework at school. Your report card will be out in a couple of weeks. Then we'll see how you're doing."

"I'm doing all right," Chuck hesitated, unsure if now was the best time. "Look, Mama, you know my old sneakers?" He paused again. "Well, they're getting a little too tight."

"Chuck, you just got those shoes this summer. Surely your feet aren't growing that fast." She continued to eat without looking up. "You want some more meat?"

"I must be growing pretty fast because those shoes are too tight. I can't run the way I should."

She shook her head. "I just can't believe they're too small this quick."

"They are. And I can't run in them. I need a new pair by Friday—for the game!"

"So that's it," she said, looking at him. "I thought you were up to something. Now I understand why you were taking the garbage down without being told. Staying home like you were civilized, for once. I knew you were after something."

"I wasn't either."

"Well, it won't do you any good anyway, even if you were. You know and I know you can't have any because there isn't any money. Those old ones will have to do until after Christmas, so you better get that out of your mind, because you're wasting your time."

"Mama," he cried, "I got to have them. You don't understand. You never understand me!"

His mother stood up and shook her finger at

him. "You better start trying to understand me. You're almost thirteen, so I know you're old enough. If I thought the old ones didn't fit, I would find a way to get some new ones. But I'm not about to do that if you don't need them. I got enough other things to find a way to get." She sat back down, exhausted.

"But, Mama, I'm going to be a game captain. I got to be good. Everybody will be looking at me. Mr. MacDonald says this is the best year our team has had a chance to beat the ninth. I can't run fast enough in those old shoes."

His mother sat quietly for a while. When she spoke her voice was calm, but there was a hint of pleading in it. "Chuck, listen to me. I understand what you're saying. You want the new ones so you can look nice for the game. I understand that. I want you to look nice too. That's one of the things I've been trying to teach you. But we don't have the extra money for something I feel you don't really need. Nobody cares how your feet look, they only care about what they can do."

It was too difficult for Chuck to hear what she was saying. "I'm telling you, I can't run in them. If I can't run, I can't play good."

"You'll have to try."

"No. If I can't have them, I'm not going to play."

"Chuck, you're going to have to grow up. You know you want to play." Her voice was firmer, but there was no sign of anger. She was trying to be patient.

"I'm not going to."

"I don't want to hear no more about it. You're the man in this house. Lord knows, I've been trying to teach you that. Being the man in this house means you have to understand what we can afford and what we can't."

They finished their supper in silence. Chuck felt there wasn't much else to say. He didn't feel like helping with the dishes, so he asked to be excused and went to his room. He sat on his bed feeling helpless. When he opened the book he was supposed to read for English, the character's problems seemed small in comparison to his own. He wanted to be a star because it must be such a good feeling. And the only way was to have shoes which would let him play at his best. They were magic, because they would let him do what he could do.

He looked at his math book, but it was even worse. Television seemed like the only thing left that could make him forget his problem. In the living room he turned on the old set that took forever to come on. When a picture finally did emerge out of the darkness, it was nothing but the President speaking. It was just too much. First his mother, then the stupid books, and now nothing on television. He would cry, if older boys and football players were allowed to.

He was already in his pajamas when he decided to give it one more chance. He went to tell his mother good night, but before he could open his mouth, she said, "The answer is still no." There was real anger in her voice this time. "You better start acting like the man in this house. You know we don't get much money. What little we do get, we need for other things. Now you think about it before you go to sleep. And good night to you, Chuck!"

"Good night, Mama." He stormed back to his room. That did it. That really got to him. He hadn't even said a word. It seemed like he couldn't even say good night to his own mother without getting jumped on. Indeed, these were his hard times.

CHAPTER SIX

The next morning the alarm went off at 6:00 as it did every school morning. Chuck lay there waiting to see if the clock would run down before his mother called in to tell him to turn it off. She had bought the clock because she didn't want him to be mad at her every morning for waking him up an hour earlier. But to Chuck it didn't make much difference. Clock or not, he still had to get up.

Why have a clock, he thought to himself as he lay there wishing he could stay in bed, at least until the sun was up. What was there to get up for? Everything was going wrong anyway. The clock ran down before he got out of bed.

"Boy, are you up in there?"

"Yes, Mama," he said, pushing the covers back.

His mother sat at the kitchen table having her coffee and listening to the radio. They exchanged good mornings when he came into the kitchen, finally dressed. As always, he wasn't going to talk much. Chuck got down a cereal bowl, got out his box of Wheaties and the jar of wheat germ. He always ate Wheaties and wheat germ for breakfast because it was good for his muscles. His mother poured herself a second cup of coffee. There didn't seem like much to say to each other.

When she finished her second cup, she turned the radio off. "Look, Chuck, I thought about what we talked about last night. Maybe the shoes are too small."

"They are, they really are!" The words came in a rush.

"Now wait. Let me finish. My check from the welfare people is supposed to come today, and if they pay me all that they're supposed to, maybe there will be some for you."

"Great! Wow, that's great! Thanks Mama. Now I'll be able to run like I really can. I'll show Craig now. Can I get them this afternoon? The game is in two more days."

"If the check comes—and keep that 'if' in mind— we can get them after school. It's supposed to have extra money in it for buying your school clothes."

Now that was the way to wake up, Chuck reasoned. Walk in the kitchen and the first thing she says is yes. Mothers sure were strange. First it's no. Then, when you think there's no hope, it's yes. All the time he was thinking, he had a great big smile on his face. Then he grabbed his mother around the neck.

"Go on, now, Chuck, and stop your foolishness." She tried to push him away, but he held on until she started to smile.

"Mama, I do need them, you'll see. I'll be the fastest thing on the team!"

"Look, Chuck, some things are hard to learn."

"I'm doing better in school." Then he added, "I even did some extra homework last night." The lie made a small gulp in his throat.

"No, that's not what I mean. I'm not talking about school learning now."

"Well, I did do some homework last night." The cereal was beginning to stick going down. He quickly added some more milk. but it didn't help.

"Boy, will you listen to me? I said it's hard to be honest with yourself. I'm talking about you telling yourself the truth."

"What do you mean?"

"Anything that's worth something is hard to understand. It's like when I was a girl, I wanted to play the piano, or at least I said I did. But I wasn't good at it. Of course I didn't tell myself I wasn't good. I would say—it's the piano, or it's the teacher. Or maybe it was because we didn't have a piano in the house. Anything, or anybody, but me. You see what I mean?"

"Well, I know I can run real fast. That's for sure!"

"Yes, I know it too. You're a good athlete. Your daddy was, and your grandfather was a big man. But you got to remember that other boys are good

31

athletes too. You can't go around waiting for a magic pair of shoes that's going to make you as fast as Superman. Do you understand what I mean?"

"Sort of, but I got to go now. Can't miss the bus." Chuck was glad to be escaping. He knew he didn't want to hear any lectures. He figured maybe that's the way parents were. Give you something, then want to lecture you about it until they feel you've paid for it.

He zipped his jacket up, grabbed his books, and started out the door.

"Bye, Chuck," his mother called after him.

"I'll see you after school, Mama," he called back, and headed for the bus.

CHAPTER SEVEN

The sun wasn't shining, but it didn't matter to Chuck, because he knew today was going to be his kind of day. Yessir, he said to himself, things were going right for a change. And it was about time. When he looked at the sky again, he didn't find the clouds threatening. They could be out if they wanted to, but they weren't going to change a thing, was his attitude.

Just 7:15, the bus was on time, and even Thelma

wasn't bugging him this morning. She was too busy talking to Diane and some of the other girls who lived in the projects. The bus stopped, the door squeaked open like an out-of-tune accordion, and everybody piled in. The bus rattled down Warren Street until it reached Dudley Station, where G.L. and Leonard got on.

"Hey, Chuck, how's your head feeling this morning?" Leonard teased. "What did your mother say about you fighting out there in that fine schoolhouse?"

"I bet she didn't know you still had to fight, at a good school too," G.L. said in a high-pitched voice. He slapped his side, and he and Leonard laughed.

"I didn't tell her. Why should I?" Chuck was willing to play along with them.

Leonard shrugged his shoulders. "I don't know. I thought you might want to tell her how you did the man in."

"So she could do you in!" G.L. added, and all three of them laughed.

"Yeah, that was some fight. That's the best I've had. I bet he won't mess with me no more," Chuck boasted between laughs.

G.L. suggested they move to the back, where they could all sit together. By that time the bus had turned off Warren Street and started for Roxbury Crossing, where it made its last stop before heading to Lexington and another day of school.

"Hey, look who just got on the bus with Brother," G.L. shouted. It was Alvin and Jimmy. They headed right down the aisle when they saw who was sitting in the back. "Wonder why they

33

didn't take the first bus like they always do," G.L. whispered.

"Who knows? And who cares? Brother rides both buses and Alvin and Jimmy ain't bothering us," Chuck whispered back.

Brother sat down two seats from the back on the right-hand side. It was a seat that would guarantee he wouldn't miss anything. Alvin and Jimmy sat on the seat in front of Chuck. They gave Chuck a hard, long look, then repeated it with Leonard and G.L. No words were spoken until the bus was almost out of the city, when Alvin turned around and said:

"You guys want to buy some protection?"

"Protection from what?" Chuck wanted to know.

"Who knows? Anything can happen. Our protection protects you from any and everything," Jimmy said while lifting his sunglasses for emphasis.

They sat awhile. Then Alvin turned around. "It's just like insurance, every bit as good as what the Metropolitan man gets your old Mama to buy. Anyway, Chuck, I heard you almost got your butt knocked off yesterday. Seems to me like you're in need of protection."

"I don't need nothing from you. I can protect myself," Chuck countered.

"And if he can't, we can," Leonard said.

"Well, don't make the mistake of thinking you three are the Black Cavalry, because you won't always be together. If I was you, I would buy me

34

some protection if I didn't want to be another Custer."

"A quarter's worth a week will go a long way," Jimmy added, lifting up his glasses again.

"Hustle your quarters from those white kids who are dumb enough to pay you, not from us," G.L. told him.

"We'll see." Alvin gave Chuck a long smile.

Brother strained his neck, his eyes, and most of all his ears, making sure he got everything down. By lunchtime everybody in the school could have an account just for the asking, and Brother could be everybody's friend. Temporarily.

"These guys think they're bad, don't they?" G.L. said when Alvin and Jimmy had walked to the front, ready to be the first off when the bus stopped. They had to make their rounds before classes started.

"I'm not afraid of them," Chuck boasted. "They're just acting like they're on TV or in a comic book. They can act that way if they want to. It's their business, and it won't be my business to pay them. What do I need protection from? Didn't I just fight the best fight of my life? Forget those guys. We ain't got time to be wasting on them."

The bus stopped. Chuck looked out the window. Every morning when he came to school he felt like he was on exhibition. It made him nervous. He wiped his sweaty palms on his pants. The other kids either walked to school or their parents drove them, and that made the dirty yellow bus with ragged seats stand out, to say the least. The bus

35

would rattle so loud that everybody and his mother would stop to look. Then the door would squeak open and everybody would stare at them as they got off. The feeling of being on exhibit would stay with him until he got back on the bus and went home.

Chuck needed to talk to Thelma about what they were supposed to have done for English. Of course, she didn't want him to see her work, but since she wanted badly to know what Alvin and Jimmy had said to him, they were able to make a little exchange.

When they went through the school doors, Chuck said to her, "Well, here we go again. Another day of being looked at like we were strange or something."

Thelma nodded. "I guess it's because we're the first ones they've seen up close."

"Don't they watch TV?"

"That's not up close, silly. That's not in person." She thought for a while. "But they'll get used to us soon. Then it won't be so bad."

"Well, just wait until Friday comes. I'm going to make so many touchdowns, they will really have something to look at. I'm going to show all of them."

CHAPTER EIGHT

That afternoon, a little after four o'clock, Chuck rushed through the front door yelling, "Did it come? Mama, Mama, did the check come?"

"Chuck, how many times have I got to tell you not to come screaming into the house like that?"

"I'm sorry, Mama, but I just had to know if it came." Chuck felt like he would rise off the floor, he was so excited.

"Well, since it's about to cause you a heart attack, I'd better tell you that it came. . . ."

"Great! Wow, when can we go get them? Can we go now?"

"If you'll let me finish. We're not going. There's been a mistake. They didn't send all the money."

"What?" There was a sinking feeling in his stomach.

"They forgot to include the clothing allowance. They were supposed to pay me back the money I spent for your school clothes. They were supposed to pay me back last month, but they didn't. Instead of paying some bills I should have paid, I went ahead and bought you the clothes. Now they've messed up again, as usual."

"What am I going to do? I need them shoes, Mama!" He felt like he was going to sink right through the floor.

"I called the welfare office. They said the computer made a mistake, and they'd send out another check," she tried to explain to him.

"When?"

"They said in a couple of days, but you know that could mean a couple of weeks. But I'm going to be checking on them this time. In fact, I'm going to check on them every day until I get my money."

Her words were of no comfort to Chuck. "A couple of days!" he shouted. "That'll be too late!"

"I'm sorry, Chuck, but there's nothing we can do but wait."

"Wait? I can't wait. The game is Friday. I need those shoes tonight."

"You're just going to have to do without them."

"But, Mama, that's not right."

"Chuck, I can't help it," his mother pleaded. "It's not my fault."

"But you promised."

"I promised because I thought they were going to send all my money. I should have known better. Those people down there don't care if we starve. Every time it's another mistake. I bet they're never making mistakes about their own money."

Chuck jammed his hands in his pockets and stalked around the room. He was trying desperately to think of what he was going to do. "Did you say they sent you something?" he asked her.

"Sure, I got the regular check. But remember, I

already skipped some bills last month. So this check has got to pay the rent, buy some food, and pay some other bills. We got to have food and we got to have a place to live. But we don't have to have a new pair of shoes for you."

"You mean *you* don't. You're not playing in the game on Friday. You're not one of the captains. I am." And he pointed to his chest.

But his mother had had enough. "Now wait a minute, young man." She started to shake her finger at him. "Let's get some of this straight. I can't let you have something if I don't have it in the first place. There's no money and that's it." His mother walked right up close to him and placed a firm hand on his shoulder. "I know one thing. If you don't stop carrying on like this, you're going to be in serious trouble."

"But, Mama, I can't run in my old ones." Chuck tried to hold back his tears.

"I told you, you could get some shoes, but I can't help it if the money didn't come! How many times do I have to tell you?" she pleaded, while shaking him.

Chuck yanked away, shouting, "But some money did come!"

Slap! Her hand flashed against the side of his face. "The money's for the rent, not for shoes. And that's the end of that. I don't want to hear no more about it." Water gathered in the corners of her eyes.

"Okay, you won't hear no more about it, 'cause I ain't going to play, and I ain't going to school tomorrow."

His mother stood with her back very straight. "Whether you play or not is up to you. Whether you go to school or not is up to me, and you will be going to school."

Chuck stormed out of the living room into his bedroom. His mother didn't call him back. He sat on the edge of his bed and complained to himself. How do you like that? First she says I can buy them, then she's saying the money didn't come. She could skip another bill, it would only be for another couple of days. It just wasn't fair.

Chuck lay on his bed for over an hour listening to his Jackson Five records, but even they couldn't help him feel better. He decided he wouldn't play. Big Mac wasn't going to like it. Neither would G.L. and Leonard. Well, that was just too bad. Craig would like it, though, you could count on that. Chuck told himself he didn't care about Craig, but at the same time he made up his mind that he wasn't through with him yet.

"Chuck?" His mother called from the kitchen. Chuck just lay there on his bed looking up at the ceiling and listening to the music. "Chuck, I know you can hear me!"

"What?"

"You come out of that room. Supper's ready. After you eat I want you to go pay a bill for me."

"I'm not hungry, and I can pay the bill tomorrow," Chuck called, and then realized he shouldn't have said that. Or maybe he should have said it another way. When his mother came in his room with her hands on her hips, he knew he had gone too far.

"Boy, what's got into you? I don't ever want to hear you talking like that to me again. When I say come and eat, that's what I mean. Come and eat! And come right now!"

"Yes, Mama. I'm coming. All I said was I wasn't hungry. That's all."

"That's not all. Now get out here and wash up for supper."

Like the night before, there wasn't much conversation. His mother was upset. Chuck was angry and disappointed. He asked if he could bring the TV in the kitchen; at least it wouldn't have been so quiet. But she wouldn't let him. After dinner Chuck helped clean up the table, even though he didn't have to.

"Chuck," his mother said as he carried some dishes to the sink, "I told you yesterday there were some things that were hard to understand, and anything that's worth something is going to be hard. You're old enough to know by now that everything doesn't work out the way you want it to."

Chuck sat at the kitchen table with his head in his hands, his eyes closed, trying very hard to understand why his mother couldn't understand.

CHAPTER NINE

That evening, right after the sun started to set and the wind off the Atlantic began to chill Boston, Chuck's mother handed him the money.

"Here's ten dollars. Tell Mr. Wilson I'll pay him the rest next week."

Chuck took the crisp green bill and held it in his hand. It was sort of funny for him, who needed money so bad, to be holding some that wasn't his. He had to give it to Mr. Wilson. There was no way. But he knew ten dollars would buy two pairs of sneakers, and all he wanted was one pair.

"Don't be standing there looking funny. Put that money in your pocket before you lose it," his mother said. She had finished the supper dishes and took down the old green book where she kept track of who she owed and how much. "You'd better go before he closes. I told him I would pay him today."

Chuck went out the door, trying hard not to think about the money. He knew that if he didn't pay the bill it would be the end of him. Yet when he was on his way, knowing the money was in his pocket, he couldn't help but think of Craig and how he needed to be better than him. Sure his mother had said things didn't always work out, but it seemed to Chuck as if nothing ever worked out for him.

So Chuck went on his way, telling himself to forget about everything he had been thinking. Mr. Wilson's store was what he had to think about. Mr. Wilson was an old man with a small store that hardly anybody ever shopped in. Just Chuck's mother and a few other older people. Most of them only bought milk and bread and other things they forgot to get at the supermarket. Most of the people went to a big supermarket up in Grove Hall. His mother said she went to the little store because at least people knew who you were. She didn't like the supermarket because nobody even knew her name.

As he walked past the big shopping center, he decided to cut through one of the stores to save time. He was just walking through when he saw the shoe department. Well, it wouldn't hurt to take a look. They even had some that would fit Big Mac's feet. You know they had to be big. They also had some that would fit Chuck's. They had the high-top kind for basketball players, and they had the low-cut kind, just like he wanted. There were black, white, red, and blue ones. He knew right away he liked the blue ones.

"May I help you?" A short woman, dressed in a green apron, who talked through her nose, was standing next to him. Without waiting for an answer, she quickly asked, "What size do you wear?"

"Nine and a half."

"What kind do you want. High tops?"

Chuck couldn't help remembering the ten dollars in his pocket. In fact, he couldn't forget it. But he knew better. "No, I don't want any. I was just looking."

"It seems like you were looking mighty hard. I bet you want a pair of red ones."

"No, blue."

"I'll have to see if we have any blue ones left. Let me see." She pulled a drawer out from under the counter. "Blue in nine and a half. Yes, here we are. They're on sale too. You're lucky. They're only three dollars and ninety cents."

"No, I'm, ah, I'm just looking." His hand was pressed tight against the money. He could feel how new that ten dollar bill felt. He looked at the shoes again. Blue was one of the school colors. A captain should have at least one of the school colors, he reasoned to himself. But he repeated to the sales-woman, "No, I can't. I mean, not right now. I'm just looking."

"You're certainly not going to find any shoes cheaper than three-ninety." She slammed the drawer closed, disappointed that she hadn't made a sale after going through all the trouble to find the right size and color.

"Maybe not, I'll look around some more." He walked away, thinking how much he wanted those shoes. Yet he felt good that he resisted buying them. But as he walked across Warren Street, he could almost feel those blue sneakers on his feet. He could see them flying down the green field. He

44

was in them, and everyone was yelling his name. Fly, Chuck, fly! He could see himself catching a pass, making a touchdown. Ah, the magic felt so good. When he reached Mr. Wilson's grocery store, the good feeling was gone and the bad feeling was back again.

As he slowly opened the door, the bell on the inside jingled. Mr. Wilson was behind the meat counter. He looked funny with his glasses down on his nose, like he was reading a book instead of making hamburger.

"Hi, Chuck. How's school? Your mother said she would send you down tonight." He smiled at Chuck as he walked over to the meat counter.

"Hi, Mr. Wilson. I came to pay our bill."

"Be right with you. I want to finish this hamburger first." Chuck watched him put big pieces of meat into the grinder. It came squeezing out in red strings of meat. Red meat that someone would make into brown hamburgers or meatloaf.

"What grade are you in now, Chuck?" Mr. Wilson was trying to find something to say.

"Eighth."

"My, my. It sure doesn't take long. I remember when you were just starting school. My, my. Time goes mighty fast, it seems like."

"It doesn't seem so fast to me."

"No, I guess not." Mr. Wilson stopped the grinder and thought about it for a minute. "When you get older, though, time has a way of getting much faster."

"I'll have to see about that," said Chuck, getting tired of waiting.

Mr. Wilson cut some more pieces of meat for the grinder. "Are you going to the King School?"

"No, I'm going to a white school out in Lexington."

"Oh, yes. I read they were taking some of the colored kids way out there. Seems like a mighty long ride. How long does it take?" He pushed his glasses up higher on his nose while he waited for the answer.

"Forty minutes."

"My, my. Just like living out in the country. That's the way things are nowadays, a little backwards. Now the kids go from the city to the country to go to school. How do you like it?" He looked over at Chuck before putting the last piece of meat in the grinder.

"It's okay." He was starting to think about school things again.

Mr. Wilson came around from behind the counter. "Now let me see if I can find your mother's bill." He fumbled through a stack of papers. "Here it is. How much do you want to pay?"

Chuck thought a minute. Did his mother tell him how much he was supposed to pay? The blue shoes flashed across his eyes. "Six dollars," he said.

"Okay, that will be six dollars, then." Chuck handed him the ten dollar bill and smiled.

Mr. Wilson looked at it. "Seems to me your mother said she was going to pay ten."

Chuck felt like he wanted to run out the door, but Mr. Wilson smiled. "Maybe it was six. I'm getting old. I can't remember anything anymore. It doesn't matter. As long as your mother has been shopping here, I know I'll get my money."

He handed Chuck the four dollars. Chuck stuffed it in his pocket, too nervous to even look at it.

"Thank you, Mr. Wilson. I got to go now. See you next week." He was out the door in a flash, with the bell jingling after him.

It had worked, Chuck told himself. He was going to have some new shoes. He quickly developed a plan. Friday was the last game. He would find a job after school. He could pay back the money before anyone found out about it. It wouldn't take long to make four dollars. Nobody would ever know. He could keep them at school in his gym locker. He would never have to bring them home.

Chuck hurried back to the shopping center. He hoped no one had bought his pair of shoes.

"So you're back," said the saleswoman with the high nasal voice. "I told you, you wouldn't find any shoes cheaper than these."

"You were right." He shoved the four dollars into her hand, still unable to look at the money. She counted it carefully.

"That was size nine?"

"No, nine and a half."

"That's right. The blue ones?"

"Yes, blue."

She wrapped them in a box and handed him his change. "You want some shoelaces? They're only a dime."

"No, the ones in the shoes will do fine."

"We have some nice colored ones. We have green and yellow and . . ."

"Do you have purple?"

"Yes, we do."

"I'll take them."

Chuck left the store whistling. He had his blue sneakers and purple laces tucked securely under his arm. Blue and purple were the school colors. He knew he was going to be looking good on the field. Chuck Walker, a game captain with blue sneakers and purple laces.

Now that he was on his way home, he had to come up with another plan. How was he going to get them in the house without his mother seeing them? There didn't seem to be many places to hide them outside. Someone might steal them. There were always too many people around just to leave them behind a tree. If he took them in the house, his mother was sure to see them. When he saw the garbage cans, he knew that was the place. Nobody would ever look in there. All the cans had names on them. Nobody ever went just looking in garbage cans. So he buried his treasure under some newspapers and put the top back on tight.

Chuck went up the steps singing. A little nervous, but singing nevertheless. Yessir. Friday was going to be his game.

CHAPTER TEN

On Thursday, Chuck found it hard to concentrate on school. It wasn't that the work was too hard, or that he couldn't do it. It was just that he was having a hard time getting interested in it. In fact, he hadn't been able to get interested in it since school started. But he promised himself that he would catch up after the football season was over.

He was making a lot of plans so his conscience would feel better. He would find a job and pay back that four dollars before his mother found out about it. He would start doing his schoolwork like he was supposed to. Since he had his shoes now, he was willing to promise himself anything. But today he found all the classes to be dragging, as if the day would never end.

Usually when the teacher called on him, he thought everybody turned around and looked at him. This bothered him and made him forget the answers, even if he knew them, which wasn't often. But today he didn't even know if a teacher had called on him. He was too busy thinking about his shoes and his troubles with Craig.

When classes finally did end, it was the time he had waited for. It was time for practice. This was the day when the game captains led the team. He hurried to the locker room and quickly dressed, putting on his shoulder pads and even his helmet before cautiously prying open the shoe box to admire his treasure.

Today was the last day of practice. There wouldn't be any contact. The coach said no team should have contact the day before a game. It was bad luck. So today was Chuck's last chance to get his pass patterns down sharp. It was also the first day the co-captains would put the team through its exercises. Craig took half the team to one end of the field and Chuck took the rest to the other end.

"One, two, three, four," Chuck shouted out as his team jumped up and down, twisting their arms and necks. From time to time he looked down at his shoes, making sure they weren't getting too much dirt on them. He put the team through twenty sit-ups for their upper stomach muscles, twenty-five push-ups for their arms, and thirty leg lifts for their lower stomach muscles. Chuck thought of the leg lifts as the most important for him, because they gave a person the power to break tackles.

The two groups joined together with a lot of noise and confusion. Big Mac blew his whistle and the talking stopped. He dropped the whistle from his mouth, and it dangled around his neck.

"Men," he said, "this is it. This is our last practice. After we finish up I want you to go straight home and get a good night's rest. And tomorrow I want you back here physically and mentally ready to play ball."

The guys on the team all started talking at once, about how they were ready right now. Big Mac had to blow his whistle to get them to shut up. "Keep it quiet in there and pay attention." He waited until he could hear them breathing. "Okay, that's better. Now remember, there won't be any contact today. I want the line down over on the south twenty yard line. The backs down there too. I want you to walk through your plays. I'll be down there in a minute or so to call the ones I want you to work on. Remember, no contact. I don't want anyone getting hurt now.

"I want the ends and the two quarterbacks on the north end. I want you to get that passing game working good. Concentrate on your down and outs and your buttonhooks. G.L., you center for them." Big Mac blew his whistle and the whole team started yelling all at once and running to both ends of the field.

At the north end, the receivers made two small lines. Craig and Adam, the second-string quarterback, took turns throwing the ball. When Chuck's turn came, he went five yards down, turned a quick buttonhook, and Adam had the ball right there. A big grin was on Chuck's face as he threw the ball back. His moves were smooth and easy, just like dancing. The magic of the shoes was working.

On his second turn he went out, turned around, but the ball bounced off his ankles. "Hey, Craig. Why don't you get the ball up, like Adam does?"

"Why don't you go out five yards, like you're supposed to?"

"Face it! You're just a lousy quarterback!"

51

"And you can't catch," Craig answered back.

Chuck went back and got in line again, waiting for his next turn. He got Adam the next time on a down and out. The ball was in front of him and he caught it. Chuck got Adam the next two times and caught the ball, though he almost dropped the last one. Somehow he managed to hang on. He even gave credit to his blue sneakers for helping his hands.

The next time up, he got Craig, and the ball went flying over his head before he could turn around good. His anger boiled up, but he said nothing or did nothing; he could see Big Mac out of the corner of his eye. The coach was coming to their end of the field. Chuck walked slowly back to the line, digging his heels into the grass. When it was his turn again, wouldn't you know it, he got Craig. He went down and out, expecting the worst. However, when G.L. centered the ball, he kept his fingers on it long enough to make Craig fumble as he backed into the pocket to throw. So they did it over. This time the ball was centered right. The ball was thrown right, but it bounced off Chuck's chest and onto the ground.

"When are you going to learn to catch, Chuck?" Craig hollered.

"Get off my back," Chuck yelled back, waiting for another turn. Big Mac blew his whistle, so there wasn't another chance to run that pattern. The team didn't do much the rest of the afternoon, just walked through some plays. But since everybody already knew them, walking through them didn't really help. Practice was finally over. Big

Mac had them run ten laps around the field before heading for the showers.

In the locker room, Chuck thanked G.L. for what he had done. Then Leonard, G.L., and Chuck had a quick shower and dressed. Chuck was putting away his equipment when the coach called him. Now what did he want, Chuck wondered. Was he going to chew him out for missing that pass?

"Come in, Chuck. I just wanted to see how you're doing," Big Mac told him as he came into the office. "How did practice go?"

"Okay, I guess," Chuck answered.

"Good. You know, I'm glad you're going to be a co-captain with Craig. I think it will help the team as well as the whole school." He paused, his face flushed. He cleared his throat. "I know it's hard for you, hard for G.L., Leonard, and the rest of you to relax out here. It's hard for all of us."

Chuck was silent. He pressed his back tighter against the locker. The room felt hot and crowded. Why couldn't the coach mind his own business, which was football, and leave mine alone, he thought to himself.

The coach mumbled on. "Of course, the whole town is talking about having black kids bused out here. It's in the papers and the kids hear it at home. It's all new to them. They're not sure how to act."

Chuck nodded.

"I'm glad you're here," Big Mac went on. "You can be good for the school. You can let us learn from you." He stopped and moved some papers around on his desk. His ears began to glow slowly, like they were real cold or raw pieces of meat. "I would be glad to have you guys here, even if you weren't playing football."

"Okay, Coach." Chuck hoped that would end their conversation, but the coach wasn't ready to stop.

"I talked to Craig. He doesn't mind being a co-captain with you."

"Sure he doesn't?" Chuck answered, looking down at the floor.

"I had a talk with him right after practice. I think things will work out."

"Okay, Coach." Chuck didn't know what else to say. Craig could say what he wanted, but that wasn't going to change the way things were when the coach wasn't around.

"Well, I guess that's something you'll have to learn in time. Anyway, I've said what I wanted to say. Let's start concentrating on the game. When I was in college, we used to call the big game War-ball, because that's what it was like, war. War with the other team and war with yourself trying to get your mind ready."

"I'm ready for any kind of war."

"Okay, Chuck. See you tomorrow. Thanks for coming in."

Chuck was relieved to get out of that hot, stuffy little office. Maybe Big Mac believed what he was saying. Who knows, Chuck wondered. Maybe he was okay, in his own way. But you couldn't tell about teachers, and you really couldn't tell about white teachers.

The locker room was empty. Chuck had to hurry if he was going to make the bus and he still had his equipment to put away. But they weren't there. They were gone. Somebody had taken his sneakers!

CHAPTER ELEVEN

Chuck continued to look. Frantically he searched under the benches, in all the unused lockers. He checked the bathrooms and the showers. No luck. His sneakers were nowhere to be found. They had vanished. He needed more time to look, but time was against him if he wanted to catch the bus. Anyway, where else could he look? He had already checked everything twice. Dejectedly he walked out of the locker room, worried about what he was going to do next.

The bus engine was running and the driver sat reading a newspaper. Chuck banged on the closed door and the driver looked up, annoyed. He checked his watch before cranking the door open. G.L., Leonard, and Thelma were sitting in the back. Before Chuck could sit down with them, the bus had jerked its way out of the parking lot.

"Man, what takes you so long?" Leonard wanted to know. "You were dressed a half hour ago."

"What ever took him so long has also messed up

his face. What happened?" said Thelma. The three of them started to laugh a little, but they stopped when they sensed that something was really wrong.

"What happened, Chuck?" Thelma asked again. "Why the ugly face?"

"Some sucker stole my shoes while I was in talking to Big Mac." Chuck took out his big silver comb and started in on his hair, ignoring the looks his friends were giving each other.

Leonard broke the silence by laughing. "You mean those old, gray, funky shoes of yours?" he teased, not knowing about the blue ones.

Thelma laughed too. She was relieved to think that nothing major had happened. However, G.L., who had been down on Chuck's end of the field, knew what was wrong. Leonard started teasing him again. "Man, you should be glad someone saved you the trouble from having to throw those funky things away." He held his nose, but G.L. stopped him before he could say anymore.

Chuck's face was tightly drawn. His lips stuck out so much they made his nose look wider. He kept combing his hair, and you could tell how he felt by the way he pulled the comb through his hair. It was as if he was trying to pull his hair out by the roots.

"Are those shoes you had on this afternoon the ones that's missing?" G.L. asked sympathetically.

Chuck nodded his head. It was difficult to speak. Leonard and Thelma shrugged their shoulders and looked at Chuck and then at G.L. It was frustrating to them not to know what was going on. As the bus moved in and out of traffic, G.L. explained that he had seen Chuck practicing in a different pair of sneakers today. That satisfied Thelma and Leonard for a while.

It was quiet, but a bit tense in the rear of the bus. On the turnpike, four sets of eyes became occupied with the cars and trucks that zipped by. There wasn't much to say or do. Each was thinking. Even Chuck was tired of combing his hair.

Leonard broke the silence in an angry, frustrated voice. "Why didn't you lock your shoes in your locker like you're supposed to?"

His anger served to release Chuck's own anger. "Because that stupid coach called me in, that's why."

"Well then, don't come around here with your mouth all stuck out. It ain't our fault they're gone."

"I didn't say it was your fault, did I?" Chuck clenched his fist.

"You should've locked them up!"

"Cool it, both of you!" G.L. urged. "There's no sense arguing with each other. We just have to figure out who's got them, then we'll get them back."

Almost before G.L. finished, Chuck shouted, "Craig! It had to be him. He must have grabbed them when I went in to see Big Mac. He must've known I was going to get called into the office."

"Yeah, that could be it. I know he had to see them when we were practicing."

Leonard, who was still upset by his exchange with Chuck, said, "Your feet are too big for him to want those shoes."

"But don't you see? He doesn't want to wear them. He's just trying to keep me from playing. He knows the only way to show me up is to stop me from playing. And I sure won't play if I don't find them."

G.L. pounded the back of the seat in front of him. "If that's the way he wants to do it, we'll just turn around and do it to him. We'll take his!"

Chuck shook his head. "No, that won't do. I have to have mine so I can run right. Besides, his wouldn't fit me, and even if they did and I wore them, he would be able to prove that I stole his, and I would be kicked off the team."

"Yeah, that's right, your feet are too big to fit in anybody's but your own," said Leonard, willing to be friendly again. The four of them laughed. Chuck was feeling a little better. "We can grab his old behind and make him give them back," said Leonard, still smiling.

The bus left the turnpike, puffed under a tunnel, and emerged up near the tall insurance building that marked the edge of downtown Boston.

When Thelma was sure the atmosphere was friendlier she asked Chuck, "What's your mother going to say about you losing your new shoes?"

Chuck was thinking so hard about getting Craig, he forgot to protect himself in other areas. "She doesn't even know I got those shoes."

"Well, how did you get the money to buy them if your mother doesn't know about them?"

"They didn't cost much. I got them on sale," he mumbled, feeling cornered.

"They must've been on sale for box tops! When did you start having money for any kind of sale? Chuck Walker, how did you get the money for those shoes?"

"I bet he ripped them off at Zayre's," Leonard offered.

"I did not!" Chuck was indignant. "I paid for them."

"They watch you pretty close in there now," G.L. told Leonard. "They even got a cop by the door to check you out."

"How much did you pay for them, then?" Thelma continued.

"Three dollars and ninety cents. I told you they were on sale," he said proudly. Then he added, "Mama gave me some money."

"But you already said she didn't know you had the shoes. Now you're telling us she gave you the money for them," Leonard quizzed.

"I didn't tell you she gave me any money for shoes!"

The three jurors all "hmmed" together.

Chuck was tired of feeling trapped, so he told them. "She gave me ten dollars to pay Mr. Wilson."

"And you only paid him. . . ."

"Six dollars."

"Ripped your own mother off?" asked G.L.

"I didn't steal nothing. I just borrowed the money. I'm going to pay it back. I didn't do any stealing. Somebody stole from me."

"It's a good thing too," added Thelma, disgustedly.

"I told you, I'm going to pay it back. I just borrowed the money. I'm going to find a job."

"Well, it sure looks like you need one. Because you still owe that money, even if you don't have anything to show for it," Leonard told him.

"Of course, if you hadn't been so busy with looking cute, you wouldn't have gotten into this mess," Thelma said, picking up her books.

"I'm telling you, I need them," Chuck pleaded. "Can't you understand?"

"I understand," said G.L. "Wanting those shoes made you steal from your own mama."

Just before the bus stopped, Chuck spoke. "You know, it wouldn't have to have been Craig. What about Alvin and Jimmy?" He was trying to forget his own guilt.

The rest were not so eager to blame the new criminals.

"They were demanding protection!" Chuck went on, trying to convince them. "Remember what they said? Protection from everything. That could mean stolen shoes."

"Could have been either of them, or Craig. Who knows?" Leonard didn't seem too interested. He and G.L. got off at Dudley without saying much more. Even Thelma didn't have a lot to say the rest of the way.

CHAPTER TWELVE

The bus pulled away from the shopping center, leaving Thelma and Chuck standing on the corner. They were surrounded by the chatter of the other kids and the honking of cars that zoomed up and down Warren Street. Thelma decided to walk home with another group of kids, and Chuck was left standing by himself. Alone. As the others walked ahead, talking and singing, trying to compete with the traffic, Chuck took out his red felt cap and pulled it tight over his carefully combed hair.

He walked along with his head down, stopping occasionally to kick at a piece of paper or a rock. The closer he came to home, the slower he walked. He even stopped to watch the bright green Cadillac, with a TV antenna coming out of the white vinyl roof.

He had seen it many times before, but today it reminded him of all the money the driver must have and what he had to do to get a green Cadillac with a TV. The conversation on the bus had made him realize what he had done, and he was in no hurry to get home and face his mother. Of course, she wouldn't know. But he knew, and he knew his knowing would make him act and feel different.

Realizing that he couldn't stay out all night, that he had to go home, he quietly unlocked the door.

"Hi, Chuck," his mother called before he could get in the house.

"Hi, Mama," he said, heading for his room.

"I'm in the kitchen, as usual. Come here. I want to talk to you."

"Okay," he answered sadly. He wasn't even going to be able to hide out in his room until he could figure out a plan.

His mother was standing over the ironing board with the iron in one hand and a can of spray starch in the other. A small burst of steam shot out of the iron. "I got a surprise for you!" She greeted him with a big friendly smile as he came into the kitchen.

"What is it?" He tried to act excited.

"I think there's going to be money left over for your shoes anyway."

"Oh," he mumbled, pushing his hands down deep in his pockets.

"Why, Chuck! What's wrong? I thought that would make you happy."

"Nothing's wrong. I just don't feel so good."

She put the iron down and placed her hand carefully against his forehead. "You don't have a fever. Does your stomach hurt?"

"Uh, a little, I think." At the touch of her hand, he wanted to tell her. He knew he had to tell her, but he couldn't find the right words.

"What's wrong, Chuck?" she asked again, pressing his head against her.

"Mama, I already got me a pair of shoes," he blurted out. He had to say it fast. If he didn't, he might not have been able to say it at all.

"What?" She lifted up his head so she could see his eyes.

"I got them last night." He confessed slowly, taking his time, since he had already told the worst part. "I only paid Mr. Wilson six dollars and I spent the rest for the shoes."

The hurt came slowly into his mother's face. First into her eyes, and then at the edges of her mouth. She pushed him away and walked over to the sink. "My Lord, my Lord," she whispered to herself as she drew water from the faucet. She poured the water into the iron and waited until the steam started to shoot from the top again. She took one of his shirts from the basket and started ironing it with quick and banging motions.

Chuck knew that ironing the collar gave her enough time to think. She always took time to think when she was hurt or angry. It kept her from doing things she would later be angry at herself for doing.

Finally she spoke. "Suppose you were standing where I'm standing, and I said I needed something or another, and you said you didn't think I needed it. But if you had the money you would get it anyway. Yet before you got time to figure out if you got the money or not, I go and get what I wanted with some money I ain't supposed to be getting it with."

The steam iron hissed and the room seemed very warm, something was simmering on the stove, adding its own steam to the room. "Mama, I'm sorry," he said helplessly, feeling like he was shrinking.

"Would my saying I was sorry be enough for you, if you were me?" She reached for another shirt.

"I don't know." His throat ached, as if there was a whole hard-boiled egg stuck halfway down, refusing to go down or up. "And somebody took them from me this afternoon." He hoped that would make her less angry.

"Good, I'm glad, Chuck, I swear to God, I'm glad, because you got them wrong, and what's got wrong, doesn't last. Boy, I tell you I don't know what I'm going to do with you." She wiped at her eyes with her sleeve. "I know one thing. You're going to pay me that money back."

"I will, Mama, I will," he promised.

"And I'll tell you what worries me. How do I know it won't happen again? So when you get bigger you'll land in jail."

Chuck held his head down. He tried to think of something to say. He wanted something good to say that would convince her that this was the first time. But by now his throat was so dry and hurting so bad, he didn't know if any words would come out at all. Then he lifted his head from the table and opened his mouth, letting the words stumble out. "If I knew you, really knew you, I would believe you." He paused for a breath of air. "Because that would be all I could do."

Mrs. Walker stopped taking down the ironing board. "Do I really know you, Chuck?"

"I don't know," he cried out, and the hurt in his throat became too much. He was too dry inside to say anything else, so he repeated, "I don't know," and laid his head back down on the table, surrendering.

Mrs. Walker looked at her son and shook her head. Then she sighed. It was her turn to surrender. "Well, I guess I'll have to believe you, even if it's hard." She said it more to herself than to Chuck.

When he looked up, she smiled at him with her eyes, and Chuck reached out. He took the ironing board from her and struggled with the latch until the legs folded together. As he put the ironing board in the closet, he swallowed, and it seemed like the first swallow he had been able to make all day. It washed the hurt from his throat. And then he knew what was on the stove. It was string beans and ham simmering in the pot; he could smell them for the first time. His mother smiled again, this time with her whole face.

Chuck said, "Thank you, Mama, thank you."

And his mother said, "Thank you, Chuck."

CHAPTER THIRTEEN

The next day started for Chuck like a big ugly clock. It jarred him awake after a night of fitful sleep. It ticked that today was Friday, his day. There were only a few hours before the game, and even fewer to find his shoes. He went to school because that was where the mystery was. Someplace in that yellow brick building his treasure was hidden. As the school bus rattled on its journey, he wished that some enormous magnet would draw him from the bus, magically taking him to the spot marked x.

All he would have to do would be to open the right door, dig in the correct spot, or climb the special tree and snatch the shoes. Of course there was no such magnet, and there were too many corridors shooting off maze-like in all directions for him to luck upon them. No, his only hope was to simply find the one who had taken the shoes and force him to reveal their hiding place. Yet even that wasn't so simple, because he would have to hunt down three possible thieves.

G. L. and Leonard were friendlier to Chuck this morning, maybe because of the nearing game. Or maybe they knew if they wanted something bad enough they might have done the same. Thelma

Chuck, who was too impatient to let them continue with their comments, demanded, "Where are my shoes?"

"On your feet." Alvin seemed surprised.

"Look, I ain't got time for your jokes. I want my shoes back."

"I don't know what you're talking about," Alvin said.

Thelma pushed her way between G.L. and Chuck. "If you got his shoes, you better tell us where they are!"

"Shut up. I've had enough from all you." And with that, Alvin shoved Thelma, who was standing the closest. She went flying into G.L., and her books scattered in the air.

Chuck shouted, "Leave her alone!" and at the same time swung at Alvin. Jimmy jumped on Leonard, but G.L. was already grabbing for Jimmy. Together they threw him against the wall, each holding one arm.

Alvin rushed Chuck, swinging his arms like an out-of-control windmill. Chuck bent down, ducking and dodging most of the blows. He got Alvin by the waist, and tried to grab his madly swinging arms. Thelma came from the left and hit Alvin on the side of the face.

"There," she said. When Alvin tried to hit back at her, Chuck threw a right jab that caught Alvin's chin, and then threw another right into his stomach.

The bell rang as Jimmy was trying furiously to yank himself free.

"I don't have your shoes," Alvin screamed. "I

don't even know what you're talking about. What shoes? Why would I take them?" He wiped at his mouth.

Leonard and G.L. released Jimmy, who rubbed his arms and straightened his shirt, staring at his two assailants.

Alvin picked himself up and started dusting off his clothes. "I don't know what this is all about, but we're not finished yet. Just remember the four of you won't always be together. And you won't always be out here in this school. I got friends at home, and I know where all of you live."

Thelma, who was frantically picking up her books and papers, which were scattered across the parking lot, lifted up her head and bit her bottom lip. "Just you remember me when you come looking," she urged.

"Don't worry, I won't be forgetting you," said Alvin, rubbing his cheek. Then he stared hard at all four of them, trying to emphasize his threat. The four stared back, and Jimmy and Alvin had no choice but to back into the school with their tough-guy image a little dusty.

"I don't think they had those shoes," Leonard remarked. "I really don't think he knew what we were talking about."

"Yeah, you're probably right," Chuck agreed, dejectedly. "Looks like it has to be Craig. And we're already late for class. What am I going to do?"

The other three shook their heads, not knowing how else to help. "We'll see Craig before the game.

The coach said he would be here then. We'll just have to get the shoes then," said G.L.

"But it'll be too late," whimpered Chuck. "If he has them at home, then he won't bring them to school. And I won't be able to play."

"Well, if you want to play, you might have to play in your old sneakers," Leonard told him. "You still have them, don't you?" G.L. and Thelma were nodding their heads in agreement.

"Yeah, but they're still old, and they haven't gotten any bigger."

"You going to let that keep you out of the game?" Leonard questioned.

Chuck pushed his tongue down into his chin. He felt tired from the fight and his side was hurting. Man, he thought, what did I ever do to deserve all of this?

Thelma and G.L. went upstairs to their class, Leonard went down to his, and Chuck went into Room 46, Problems in Social Studies. He repeated to himself, What did I ever do to deserve this?

CHAPTER FOURTEEN

Everybody in school was talking about the game, except Chuck. He sat in each of his classes thinking about what he was going to do next. In a way there wasn't much to think about. The game was so important to him he couldn't miss it. But what kept him thinking, what kept his mind going faster and faster, was trying to figure out how he was going to get those shoes from Craig before the game.

The morning went slowly. The waiting got harder and harder. When lunchtime finally came, Chuck hurried to the cafeteria just in case Craig came back early. No luck. Chuck picked over his peas and salad, trying to think of a way to find Craig. By the time he convinced himself he would need a car to get to Craig's house and back, lunch was over.

Back to his classes. Time got slower. Every time he checked the clock, the hands had barely moved. The rest of the school was getting excited because they were getting out an hour sooner. Even the teachers forgot about teaching and allowed free reading.

The only problem with free reading was that every class had the same magazine. The *National Geographic* with pictures of half-dressed women. Chuck thumbed through the pages, wondering about his shoes. From time to time he wondered if that's how Thelma looked.

During the few moments when he was convinced that the clock had moved, he would repeat to himself what he was going to do with Craig. When it was at last two o'clock, the assistant principal, Mr. Carlton, announced over the loudspeaker, "All those participating in this afternoon's football championship are excused from class."

Chuck sprang from his seat. He was the first one

out the door, heading straight for the gym. He didn't stop and wait for Leonard and G.L., like he had promised. There wasn't time. His walk was brisk and determined. His arms pumped up and down, and he held his head very straight and forward. As he hurried, the veins and muscles in his neck were ready to pop out. When he reached the gym, he broke through the door like a sprinter breaking the tape. Craig was sitting on the bench putting on his socks, with his back to the door. Chuck headed straight toward him. The closer he got, the faster he moved, until he leaped in the air and grabbed a surprised Craig around the neck. They both fell to the floor.

"What's wrong with you?" Craig yelled.

Before Chuck could say anything, Big Mac came running out of his office and reached down and grabbed Chuck behind the neck with his thumb and fingers and jerked him to his feet. "Damn you two! Are you trying to lose the game for me, fighting like this, and the game about to start?"

"It wasn't my fault," said Craig. "I was sitting here and he jumped on me. I didn't even see him."

"He took my new sneakers!" Chuck yelled.

"I didn't," argued Craig.

Big Mac looked confused and worried. Time was running out for him. He scratched his face and looked at his watch. "What kind of shoes were they, Chuck?"

"Blue ones, with purple laces. I just bought them. And he took them after yesterday's practice," Chuck said, pointing to Craig.

"Craig, do you know anything about them?" Big Mac asked. Craig shook his head and looked at him.

"No, Coach, I don't. I saw them yesterday. He had them on. I haven't seen them since. I swear I didn't take them, Coach."

Big Mack scratched his hairy arms this time. "Well, Chuck, I don't know what to say. Did you check with the janitor? Maybe you left them out or something." Chuck shook his head no. "Well, there's no time now. Do you still have your old ones?"

Chuck held his head down his eyes big and cloudy. "Yes, but they don't fit."

"Well, they'll be better than nothing. I want to know if you two are going to be able to play together." He bent down, pointing his finger at Craig and Chuck. It was as if he was about to take a shot at them. "I'm not going to let you two lose a game that I know you can win." His face was bright red and his eyes were also bright. "Now I tried do what I thought might help, letting you both be captains. But still you're not willing to work together. If I have to, I'll sit both of you on the bench!"

Big Mac pulled himself up and saw the rest of the team standing around, listening and watching him. "What are you standing around looking dumb for? Get dressed and out there on that field before I send all of you home!" he yelled at them. Then he headed for his office, taking giant steps as if to make up for lost time.

Craig sat back down and started to put on his

sock again. He looked up at Chuck, who was still standing near him. "Chuck, you're crazy. You know that, don't you?"

"Shut up, Craig, I don't have to take any lip off of you! I know you got my shoes."

Craig shook his head. "You're wrong. I really don't have them."

"Where are my shoes, Craig?" Chuck pleaded.

"Chuck, believe me, I don't have them." Craig stood up. "We better think about how we're going to win this game."

"You think about it." Chuck stood there for a moment more, hesitating. He wanted to do something to get even. He thought about grabbing Craig's sock, but that wasn't enough. There wasn't anything he could do. Instead he turned around and walked away. His shoulders bent inward and seemed to hang lower.

He walked back to his locker and sat down on the narrow bench. He said nothing to Leonard and G.L., who were just about dressed. They could see it was best not to say anything to him. Chuck watched them dress, as he sat there, not moving. But by the time they were finished, Chuck gave in, because he knew there was nothing else for him to do but play. He had allowed the game to mean too much to him, and because it meant so much, he couldn't let it slip away now.

By the time G.L. and Leonard left, Chuck had quickly slipped into his pants and was adjusting his thigh pads. Then he tightened the straps of his shoulder pads and stuck his head into his game jersey. He lifted his old shoes from the bottom of his locker and stared at them. They were still dirty. The tear on the side was still there. He sighed and put the left one on. He wiggled his toes around. It didn't seem too tight! He laced up, and it still didn't seem too tight. He put the right one on, and it seemed to be all right too.

"Hmmm," he murmured, and wiggled both feet. "Hmmm. Maybe they're not as tight as I thought." Then he reached for his helmet and started for the door.

CHAPTER FIFTEEN

Craig stood waiting for Chuck on the other side of the door. "Chuck," he said. "I've been thinking about what the coach said. Have you?" There were large nervous spaces between his words. He seemed uncertain whether he should continue.

Chuck leaned against the wall, gently banging his helmet against his right leg. It was hard for him to be standing there, feeling the way he did about Craig. Yet the game was so close, and his old shoes didn't seem to fit so bad.

"A little," he answered.

The two captains stood in the hallway talking

to each other for the first time. The rest of the school was emptying out of its classrooms and filling the hall with chatter, laughter, and mostly noise.

"I guess we both want to win this game. Don't we?" Craig paused. "So I've been thinking about how we've been acting to each other." Craig shifted his weight from one foot to the other. "You know we've both been wrong?"

"Maybe," Chuck mumbled.

"Come on, will you? It just can't be all my fault?"

"What've I done?" Chuck started to bang his helmet harder against his leg.

"How about just coming in and jumping on me? I didn't do anything to you."

"Yeah, but I thought you had my shoes." Chuck's voice became louder. "I don't know who has them, if you don't!"

"Well, I told you, I don't."

"Well, just tell me why you've been throwing the ball either over my head or under my feet."

Craig shifted his weight once again and frowned. "Okay, okay, that was my fault. But you were acting like a big hero all the time. I was trying to show you that if it wasn't for me throwing the ball, you wouldn't be such a hotshot."

"To me, you're the one who thinks he's Mr. Pro Quarterback. Everyone thinking you were so great," Chuck added with special bitterness. "If it wasn't for me catching the ball, you wouldn't be nothing."

"You're just jealous, that's all."

"No, you're the one," Chuck blinked his eyes as if he had been slapped. Craig's words had hurt him, and he wasn't sure why. He wanted to hurt back, but there was nothing else to say.

"Maybe I was." Craig continued to shift his feet. "But if we're going to win this game, then you and I have to get along."

"All you have to do is throw the ball right. I'll catch it fine."

"And all you have to do is block sometimes. Do you ever think about blocking?" Craig pointed his finger at Chuck. "Just once let me see you throw a decent block! Remember, we can't throw the ball all the time. We've got to run it too. You need to block for the runners and that includes Leonard!"

"Don't come preaching to me. You trying to say I can't block?" Chuck slapped Craig's finger away.

Craig's hand automatically became a fist when Chuck slapped at him, but then he relaxed his hand and unfolded it. He stopped what he was about to say and instead said, "No, that's not what I mean. I'm just trying to say, we've got to work together."

By now all the classes had emptied into the hallways. The students flowed by Craig and Chuck, shouting encouragement to them. With each "Hello" or "Go get 'em" the captains' eyes sparkled more and more. The crowd was making them feel good. The excitement of the game flooded over them, and they forgot about their argument, a little. Putting on their helmets, they walked with the crowd, feeling that they had already won the game.

"Chuck," Craig said when they were outside, "I've thought of a plan. It will fool everybody."

"What is it?" There was suspicion in Chuck's voice.

"Well, everyone knows that we throw to you a lot, right?"

Chuck nodded, then shrugged. "What's so new about that?"

"That's just it. They'll be expecting it."

"That's okay. I'll get in the open." Chuck felt confident.

"No, I've got a better idea. I won't throw to you as much."

"What?" Chuck's suspicion was growing. "Are you trying to hog everything up again?"

"No, this will be different."

"Sure it will. It'll be different because you want me to block all the time, instead of scoring points."

"No! Listen, will you? We'll run an end around. Just like Miami does with Warfield. You come around the right side. It's something we've never done before. Nobody will be looking for it, not even Big Mac."

"Look, I ain't going to be blocking for you all the time, just to carry the ball once."

Craig stopped walking and looked at Chuck. "I want to win," he said. "And I think this could be a big play. Besides, I'll be throwing to you sometimes, but not as much, that's all."

"Sounds like a trick to me."

"It's not, either. You'll see."

It was Chuck's turn to look at Craig. "Okay, we'll do it. And it better not be a trick."

"It won't." Then Craig added, "I'm sorry about the fight." He offered Chuck his hand.

Chuck rubbed his fingers with his thumb, keeping his hand close to his side. "Me too," he mumbled slowly. Then he pried his hand away from his side and shook Craig's hand.

CHAPTER SIXTEEN

It was game time. And the game captains, Craig and Chuck, went to the center of the field for the flip of the coin. Mr. Willard, a history teacher, gently tossed the coin in the air. The ninth-graders called tails; Chuck and Craig called heads. The coin came down, flashing against the sun and landed tails up. The ninth chose to receive. They were anxious to get their offense rolling. On the sides of the field, the teams ganged around their coaches.

"Okay, men!" Big Mac yelled with his hands on his hips. His players had their arms around each other's shoulders. Up and down they started to jump, becoming with each jump a giant pogo stick. Chuck's heart was going faster and faster. This was what he had been waiting for. All the other things were washed from his mind. There was only the game.

"This is it," Big Mac yelled in the center of the bouncing ring. "We can do it. Let's get out there and show them just how!"

"YEAH TEAM!" the players responded. And, as if on cue, Mr. Price's ninth-graders broke up their circle with a big yell. So Big Mac had his players holler again before sending the starting players charging onto the field.

The weather was just right; a little cool, but with lots of bright sunshine. It was a good day for football. Chuck could see the people in the stands. Some parents had come, but not his mother. They lived too far away. He wished she could see him in his old shoes now that they were fitting again. He wanted her to see how well he was going to do. He found Thelma sitting with Diane. When he was sure she was looking, he started running vigorously in place, making sure his legs were ready.

Chuck's heart was beating faster and faster. Mr. Willard blew the whistle. G.L. held the ball, and Johnny, the team's best kicker, was ready to kick off. The line stood still waiting. Johnny started his slow, easy trot. Just as he passed the line his legs churned faster, and the rest of the team started their trotting. Johnny's right foot went back, and then he quickly punched the ball with his toe, kicking it up and out.

His team was now following the ball as fast as they could. It traveled high in the air and then floated down into the arms of number 42, who started running against the runners. He was at the fifteen, the twenty, the twenty-five. Then the two teams met at the twenty-six yard line with the bumping and slamming sounds of bodies and equipment. Number 42 went down. The sidelines sprang up with a loud roar. From somewhere in the pile, Chuck pulled himself up. Craig had fallen next to him, so he helped him up. Chuck's heart wasn't beating fast now. The game had started, and he was relieved.

On the first series of downs, the eighth grade held the ninth for three plays. The ninth grade punted. On the first play, Craig called the signals. On the count of two, Leonard tore out of his stance, tucking the ball safely in his arms, and went slamming off-tackle. He made only one yard. The next call up the middle went nowhere, and on the third down an incompleted pass forced Johnny to come in and punt. Chuck was beginning to feel tired. He was trying his best to block, but these guys were bigger and harder to move than the eighth-graders. The two teams had tested each other and had only proved there was a lot more testing to be done.

The punt was a good one. It was high and deep, sending the ninth-grade team way back to their own territory. It was high enough to prevent a runback. But they came out of their huddle yelling, determined to move the ball. Chuck got ready. He looked at number 42. He was their best player, and Chuck knew they were going to have to try to bury that number under a pile of purple shirts every time he got the ball.

On the first play, their quarterback, who was

also a good passer, hit on a quick pass for five yards. That gave them confidence, and they came out of the huddle yelling again. Two more yards down the middle and on the third down, number 42 took the ball off-tackle and went eight big yards. They had made the first down of the game, and they were willing to keep that pattern going. Chuck dug in. He preferred to play offense, but he knew that today he was going to have to play his best defensive game if he hoped to have a chance of getting his hands on the ball again.

The ninth-graders were beginning to feel their power. On each play they came running out of their huddle faster and yelling louder. Number 42 got the ball again and ran for five yards on the right side. Their fullback went for two yards and a successful pass gave them their second first down. Soon they had marched the ball to the eighth grade's thirty-five.

On the next play their quarterback faked to the running back, going into the line and then running a keeper around Chuck's end. Chuck charged for the ball carrier. He could see number 42 trailing behind the quarterback, ready for a lateral. He left his feet and grabbed the quarterback's arms just as he was tossing the ball backwards. The ball bobbled up, hung in the air between Chuck and number 42, and bounced on the ground. Instead of scrambling for the ball, Chuck moved his body between number 42 and the ball, blocking him. A purple shirt pounced on it. The eighth had stopped them.

"Good going, Chuck," G.L. said in the huddle.

"You probably stopped a touchdown." The rest of the team agreed.

"It was just luck," he said, pleased with himself. "But we got to get going!"

Three plays later, they had moved the ball only nine yards and had to punt again. The two teams fought evenly for the rest of the quarter, and when it ended, the score was 0-0. Everybody could see that the game was going to be hard. Whoever could stand the pressure would win.

The second quarter started off much better. Craig decided to keep the ball. He sprinted out to his left. Chuck charged out of his stance, throwing his body sideways across his man. It was a good block. Craig scampered around Chuck's end for six yards. With each block Chuck threw, it seemed as if his body ached more. Yet as each block stopped his man, the more he felt like blocking.

The ninth grade's defense tightened up on the next play and held the running back for no gain. Third down and four; it was a passing down. Chuck knew it had to be a passing play, and he wanted the ball to come to him. And a pass play it was, but to the other end. Chuck bit the inside of his mouth hard as he came out of the huddle. On the count, the ball was snapped. Chuck bumped his man like he was supposed to, and then moved down the field running his decoy pattern. He didn't bump his man very hard or move very fast. It was too tiring. He knew he was only the decoy and not Craig's first choice, and he began to lose his drive to run as fast. He comforted himself by thinking he had to save his power until he was sure the ball was coming his way.

The pass was completed for the first down. The mood in the huddle was picking up. Craig clapped his hands. "We got 'em now!" he said. Chuck was silent, moving his foot back and forth over a clump of grass as Craig called the next play. With the plays being called so fast and everybody else co-operating, Chuck had to go along with the way Craig was doing things, at least for the time being. He was beginning to feel trapped. It seemed that all of his blocking and tackling was just going to make Craig look good. He wanted some attention for himself, and the only way was to score a touch-down.

The next play was another pass, this time to Leonard. It went for twelve yards. They were past the fifty yard line for the first time. Everything seemed to click after those two plays. Craig mixed up his plays well. He came back with two running plays and a pass play, followed by three running plays and then a daring draw play that sent Leonard slamming and busting over two would-be tacklers. He scored. It was 6-0, and the eighth-graders on the field, on the bench, and in the stands were jumping and hollering.

Chuck slapped Leonard's hands. He was glad that Leonard had been the one to score, but as he listened to the crowd, he couldn't help but remember that he was supposed to be the one to make everyone cheer. And he couldn't help but think that if just one of those passes had been to him, he would've scored. But he fought to keep those thoughts to himself. At least his team was winning. That's what matters, he repeated over and over to himself, trying to believe it.

They failed to run the ball in for the extra point, and it was still 6-0. The ninth grade came back mad that they had been scored on. They gave the ball to their best player every chance they got. It was number 42 up the middle, then around the right side, then back up the middle. He even caught the ball once. But their attack wasn't balanced. Although they moved the ball well enough to pick up the first three downs, Chuck began to know how number 42 moved his head when he was going to run around his end. The more Chuck anticipated the more aggressive he became. Soon he had thrown their star runner for a three-yard loss. The ninth couldn't get their offense going after that loss.

At the end of the first half, the eighth grade had a surprising lead. Chuck was relieved when he heard the gun. He was exhausted. Now he could understand why the pros only played offense or defense. As he headed off the field dragging his helmet, he was disappointed that he hadn't caught a pass, but pleased that he was playing such a good defensive game.

CHAPTER SEVENTEEN

At half time the teams stayed on the field. The eighth went down to the south goalpost. The other team went to the north end. Big Mac stood in the middle of his players.

"We're doing okay. Right now they're surprised they can't score on us. We're holding good on defense. This is the best I've seen you on defense."

Chuck wanted to smile, but he was too tired to exercise even his face muscles. He rested and thought about Craig, wondering if he was trying to trick him or not. He hadn't thrown to him yet, not even a short one. Big Mac's voice flowed back to Chuck.

"Keep on the pressure and try to get some more points on the board. That's a good way of keeping the lead." There was a few half smiles, but the team was too serious for very much humor. Yeah, Chuck thought to himself, Craig's going to have to throw it my way; at least that would be a way of mixing up the pass plays. Big Mac was winding up. "Remember, play the same kind of defense, but try to get a few more touchdowns. Any questions?" There were none. "All right, on your feet. It's time."

The weary team pulled itself up slowly. When all the players were up, they gave their yell. It wasn't as loud as before. They were trying desperately to save their energy for the second half.

"Hey, Craig," Chuck called. "When are we going to do that play?"

Craig snapped his helmet strap. "I sure fooled them the first half, didn't I? They kept waiting for me to throw to you."

"Well, you didn't fool them by yourself. And I think they're fooled enough and I'm ready. So you can call it soon, before you forget it!"

Craig yanked his helmet off. "Look, I'm the quarterback. I'll call what I want to, when I want to. We're winning aren't we? So I'm doing all right."

"I told you, you ain't doing it by yourself, you know? We're all in it! And if you don't start throwing to me, and call my play, you better get ready to take the ambulance home."

"Look, wise guy, you think I'm scared of you? Well, I'm not."

"You want to win this game, or not?" Chuck trotted away before getting an answer.

The ninth grade kicked off. The ball went to Craig, who started running up the middle. The line moved to the middle, setting up a wall. Then he cut to his left and came around Chuck's end. Number 51 moved up to make the tackle. Chuck dropped his shoulder and hit him just below the knees, sending him flying, but he still managed to reach out and pull Craig down on the thirty-three.

"Why didn't you block that guy?" Craig asked him as they walked back to the huddle.

"What?"

"You heard me!"

"Just shut up, will you, before you get blasted right in your stupid mouth. I did the best I could. I hit him, didn't I?"

"Yeah, you hit him all right. You knocked him right into me." It was Craig's turn to walk away before the conversation was finished. He left Chuck feeling hurt and angry.

The third quarter quickly became like the first. A hard, tough, evenly fought game. It was difficult for either team to make enough yardage. No one made a first down. It was three plays and punt matched by three plays and punt. With only three minutes to go in the quarter, Craig called for Chuck to cut across the middle and go deep.

"About time," Chuck commented.

"Just shut up and play, will you?" Craig answered.

G.L. spoke up. "Come on, you two, don't start arguing now."

Chuck listened to him because he knew he was right. So he kept his thoughts to himself. On the line he watched G.L. settle over the ball.

Craig called, "Ready, set!" The line set. "Hut one, hut two, hut three." Chuck went down five yards, faked his head to the left, turned right, and broke away into the clear. Craig threw the ball to the other end, and it was batted down.

That was just too much to take. Chuck flung his

arms in the air and walked slowly back to the huddle, mad. Not knowing if he wanted to walk right up to Craig and slam his helmet in his nose, or walk off the field and go home, he demanded, "Man, I was clear. Why didn't you throw it to me?"

"I didn't see you. I was rushed." Craig's face flushed. The pressure of the game and his words with Chuck were beginning to show on his face.

"Well, you better start opening your eyes." Chuck decided that was enough to say for now. He would wait to finish it after the game. The score was still 6-0 at the end of the third quarter.

The fourth quarter found both teams near exhaustion. Neither coach substituted much. Each wanted to win. But somehow the ninth-graders seemed less tired. They started hammering out small pieces of yardage. Then it started to build up to first downs. They moved the ball to the forty-five, and then over the fifty. They kept pounding away until they were on the twenty yard line.

Chuck wanted badly to stop them. He dug in, determined to break through like he had done before. Their quarterback took the snap from center and moved back with the ball like he was going to throw. Then he pitched out to number 42, who started going around the other end.

There was nothing Chuck could do. G.L. had busted through and got the quarterback, but he had already gotten rid of the ball. Number 42 just danced and dodged through purple arms. And those he couldn't dance through or his blockers couldn't block, he ran over. Someone grabbed him

90

at the two, but he fell over for the touchdown, and his teammates ran around and hugged him. They were back in the game. Their excitement lasted until they failed to run in the extra point. It was still 6-6.

The game was still tied with only two minutes to go. The eighth had the ball on their own forty-five. In the huddle, everybody was tired and tense.

"Chuck, end around on five," Craig said.

Chuck stiffened when he heard the play. This was it, and they needed a touchdown.

"Let's see if you can do something besides run your mouth," Craig added.

Chuck said nothing. Instead he wiggled his toes to make sure his shoes were still fitting.

G.L. was over the ball. "Get set," Craig called. Chuck dug his knuckles on the ground and his feet in. "Hut one, hut two, three, four, five." Chuck dropped back, crossing through his backfield. Craig handed him the ball, he faked like he kept it, running hard into the line. Chuck went around to the other side.

"REVERSE!" The other team called.

But by then Chuck was past the fifty yard line, cutting to the outside and picking up his blockers. Jumped over one tackler on the forty-nine. Got a good block at the forty-five. Cut back to center. Tripped up at the thirty-five but stayed on his feet. Moved to the right and got another good block at the twenty-five. Then he turned on the speed. And he was all alone. Across the goal for six points. Chuck threw the ball down, just like he had seen players do on TV. The sidelines were going wild.

He could see Thelma jumping up and down and shaking her head from side to side. The whole team piled up on him, banging him on the head until his helmet was ringing.

"That was a good run, Chuck," Craig said, smiling.

"That was a good fake into the line. They really thought you had the ball." Chuck was smiling too.

"Yeah," said Craig. "It was a good play. Looks like we're going to win."

"It sure was, and it sure does," Chuck said, and slapped Craig's open hand.

They didn't make the extra point, but were able to hold on for the last minute. The clock stopped. The gun went off. The game was over.

CHAPTER EIGHTEEN

After the game, the team was feeling delirious. The delight of winning became too much. They wanted to carry Big Mac off the field, but as soon as a few grabbed his legs, they realized they would be lucky to carry their own helmets. Big Mac was delirious too. It was his first win over one of Mr. Price's teams in five years. He even promised to treat the team to hamburgers and Cokes on Monday.

Craig and Chuck stood facing each other in a new and strange way. Deep inside they were still mad at each other. Too much had happened to be erased and forgotten in one play.

"I guess I've been arguing with you because I've been worried about the game," Craig said as they waited for a drink of water in the locker room.

"Well, I guess I've been worried about it too," Chuck said, getting a drink. "You know, your fake helped set up that touchdown."

"No, it was your running that got us the touchdown," Craig insisted.

They stood there with the water fountain between them, speaking words that were hard to say and didn't feel right. Yet they were words which were influenced by winning, and by the celebration noise. Chuck wanted to ask why Craig had waited so long to call the play. Was it because there were only two minutes left, and things looked so desperate that he was willing to try anything?

As the congratulations filled Chuck's ears, he realized it was a question he wouldn't ask now. He would save it and ask it another time.

"Chuck," Big Mac called. "Chuck, I think I found your shoes. Are these the ones?" He held out a pair of size nine and a half blue sneakers with purple laces.

"Yes," Chuck answered, "Those are mine. Where did you find them?"

"They were on my desk with a note from the custodian saying he found them under a locker."

Chuck took his shoes and held them up and remembered how good they were going to make him look, and how fast they were going to make him run. Their magic was gone now. He had run as fast as he could in the old ones, and he knew the new ones couldn't have been any faster. He wiggled his toes, knowing he would have looked good in the blue shoes with purple laces, but there was no magic in them now. The magic was in him.

"I'm glad you found your shoes, Chuck," Craig offered.

"Yeah, me too." Chuck wondered how they got under a locker. Had Craig done it, or had he dropped them himself and somehow kicked them under there? He didn't know, and probably never would know.

"Well, I'm going to get dressed. I guess I'll see you Monday." Craig started to walk away, but turned and said, "Hey, maybe you can come over my house sometime."

"Why don't you come over to mine?" Chuck suggested.

"I don't know. Roxbury is so far."

"So is Lexington!" Chuck countered.

"Yeah, I guess you're right. Well, I'll catch you Monday." And the two captains went to their lockers.

Later, on the bus which was noisier than the locker room, Chuck sat in the back with Leonard, Thelma, and G.L. They were all glad the weekend was coming. Glad to be together. Glad to sit back in the raggedy seats and relax. When Thelma saw the shoes, she wanted to know what he was going to do about them.

"What do you think? Take them home?" Chuck told her.

"No, I mean how are you going to pay your mother back?"

"I don't know yet. I'll think of something."

"I got an idea," G.L. said. "We can go over to the supermarket and carry groceries. Saturdays are always busy over there.

"The three of us could make four dollars in no time," Leonard said.

"And I could help too, or I could lend you some of my typewriter money, Chuck," Thelma offered.

"No," said Chuck, taking his comb out of his pocket. "This is something I got to do myself."